# the runawæ chimps

*by Cathrine Barr*

**NEW YORK**
**HENRY Z. WALCK, INCORPORATED**

Minerva wos wun ov the for littl chimpanzees hœ livd at the zœ. ∫hee and her sisters plæd aull dæ.

the gæest ov her sisterrs wos Molly.

the uther tʍ wer kæt and bʍ, and
thæ wer jolly and fʍll ov fun.

Wun dæ whiel Mac, the zω keeper, wos cleenig up,

Minni and her sisters sneekt out ov thær cæj.

as fast as thæ cωd run, the for littl chimps left
the zω and went up the stræt.   .   .   .

. . . and riet intw the cloething stor.

Whot fun þæ had trieiŋ þiŋs on! When þæ left
þe stor eech littl chimp wos wæriŋ whot ʃhee liekt best.

tha wer aull dresst up, but had noe plas tw goe.   .   .

. . . until the that ov goeing tw the mœvis.

after the ſhoe thæ wer hungry, soe thæ helpt
themselvs tω ies creem whiel the ies creem man
had his back turnd.

Jhæ strutted up the street, licking the ies creem, and marcht riet in frunt ov the polees offiser.

hee gæv them a ʃharp lʊk as hee held up the traffic.

but thæ went riet aloŋ, hediŋ tʊwaʊrd the park.

Nun ov the peepl ho hurrid past noetist the chimps,

for thæ we∕r well disgiesd in thær snappy cloeths.

Suddenly, at the corner nuesstand,
thæ sau the enormus hedlien .  .  .  .

. . . . . chimps hav run awæ!

thæ nue thæ wer sæf, for hœ wœd recogniez them
in thær fien clœths? Sœ thæ stoppt tœ reed
the story, and lernd thær keeper had

been put in jæl for lettiŋ them escæp. thæ
rememberd hou nies hee had been tω them
and desieded tω visit him.

Sœ thæ hurrid tw the jæl . . . . . .

and thær wos Mac, lockt up tiet and lwkiŋ very unhappy.

but Minni and her sisters had tw laf.
thæ laft and laft.

It wos very funny tu see thær keeper behiend the bars.

Soon thæ stoppt lafiŋ becaus thær
œld frend, Mac, lʊkt sœ sad.

þæ nue whot þæ ſhcvd dœ. Yes, þæ
turnd themselvſ in, sœ þær keeper cvd gœ free.

And Minni and Molly, kæt and bɷ went riet back tɷ the zɷ, back behiend the bars.

but thæ wer happy. . .thæ wer hœm,
and Mac wos free.

the runawæ chimps had lernd
that hœm is the best plæs tw bee.